FOR JEANNETTE —D. R.

MARGARET K. McELDERRY BOOKS

An imprint of Simon & Schuster Children's Publishing Division

1230 Avenue of the Americas, New York, New York 10020

Text copyright © 2010 by Douglas Rees

Illustrations copyright © 2010 by Olivier Latyk

MARGARET K. McELDERRY BOOKS is a trademark of Simon & Schuster, Inc.

For information about special discounts for bulk purchases, please contact
Simon & Schuster Special Sales at 1-866-506-1949 or
business@simonandschuster.com.

The Simon & Schuster Speakers Bureau can bring authors to
your live event. For more information or to book an event, contact
the Simon & Schuster Speakers Bureau at 1-866-248-3049 or visit our
website at www.simonspeakers.com.

Book design by Debra Sfetsios

The text for this book is set in Ad Lib ICG.

The illustrations for this book are sketched in pencil and then rendered in Photoshop.

Manufactured in China

0210 SCP

10 9 8 7 6 5 4 3 2 1

Library of Congress Cataloging-in-Publication Data

Rees, Douglas.

Jeannette Claus saves Christmas / Douglas Rees; illustrated by Olivier Latyk.—1st ed.

p. cm.

Summary: When Santa falls sick on Christmas Eve, his feisty daughter, Jeannette, takes his
place in the sleigh and saves the day, despite rebellious reindeer.

ISBN 978-1-4169-2686-3 (hardcover)

1. Santa Claus—Juvenile fiction. [1. Santa Claus—Fiction. 2. Reindeer—Fiction. 3. Christmas—
Fiction.] I. Latyk, Olivier, ill. II. Title.

PZ7.R25475Je 2010

[E]—dc22

2008023021

FIRST EDITION

Jeannette Claus
Saves Christmas

by **Douglas Rees**

illustrated by
Olivier Latyk

MARGARET K. McELDERRY BOOKS
New York   London   Toronto   Sydney

SANTA CLAUS was sick.

He **sneezed.**

He **coughed.**

He **groaned.**

He **moaned.**

He **sniffled**

and he

blew.

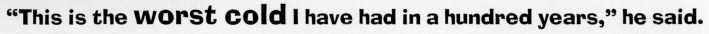

"This is the **worst cold** I have had in a hundred years," he said.
"And I have to deliver presents tonight."

His daughter, Jeannette, brought him another

cup of herbal tea.

"Jumping jingle bells, there is **no way** I am letting you take the sleigh out tonight," she said.

"I'll do it."

"You don't know what you're talking about," said Santa. "Those reindeer are **tricky.** They **hate** hauling me around on Christmas Eve. Dasher's the worst. If he had his way, no one would get any presents."

"If I can handle you, I can handle eight tiny reindeer," Jeannette said.

"I'm not going to let you do it," Santa said. **"It's my job."**

Then he **sneezed.**

He **sneezed** again.

He **exploded** in sneezes.

"You're right," he groaned.
"I can't make it. You'll have to go.

"The job's easy, really," Santa said. "Just remember two things. Always say, 'On Dasher, on Dancer, on Prancer and Vixen. On Comet, on Cupid, on Donner and Blitzen.' Otherwise the reindeer can't fly. And be careful to keep their harness tight. If they get loose, you're stranded."

So Jeannette went out to the barn and loaded the sleigh. Then she took down the harness and laid it out.

"All right, you guys," Jeannette said to the reindeer.
"Time to rock and roll."

"You're not Santa," Dasher said.
"You're not Santa," Dancer agreed.
"You're not Santa and we don't have to go out,"
said Prancer, Vixen, Comet, Cupid, Donner,
and Blitzen.

"Criminy Christmas
crackers," Jeannette said.
"Don't give me a hard time.
We've got work to do."

One by one she dragged the reindeer over to the harness and buckled them in.

"Merry Christmas—here we come!" she shouted.
"On Dasher, on Dancer, on Prancer and Vixen. On Comet, on Cupid, on Donner and Blitzen."

Up, **up** they rose.

The stars came **closer** and **closer.**

The air grew **colder** and **colder.**

When the reindeer spiraled down to land on the nearest roof, Jeannette jumped out of the sleigh, slid down the chimney with a sack of presents, and popped up again in a minute.

"Nothing to it," she said. "We'll have this job done in no time."
On through the night she sped, calling to the reindeer and dropping through the chimneys.

Around the world she and the reindeer flew. Everything was going exactly right.

"We may get done early. If we do, it's extra oats for all hands."
The reindeer didn't answer.

Then, as they were setting down on top of a building, the pin that connected the harness to the sleigh fell out.

"**Suffering sugarplums,**" Jeannette cried as the sleigh hit the roof with a bump.

"Dash away, dash away, dash away, all!" cried Dasher, and the eight reindeer flew away with their harness bells jingling.

"Come back here, you stupid hat racks!" Jeannette shouted. But the reindeer didn't even look back. The sleigh was still more than half full of presents.

This was terrible. A world full of people were waiting for her sleigh. She paced up and down under the cold sky, trying to think of an idea, but nothing came to her.

Down below
in the alley,
she heard a noise.

A dog was down there. He looked sad and hungry.
"Poor pooch," Jeannette said. "Cold and starving on
Christmas Eve." She slid down the drainpipe and went over to him.

She scratched him behind the ears.

"Have you got a name?"
"Guess you can call me Rover. Roving's about all I do."

There was a soft little meow behind them.

"Come on over here," Jeannette said, and picked up a small black cat.

"I'm Caesar," the cat said. It started to purr.

Now the shadows were full of cats and dogs.

"I'm Blaster," said a big orange tomcat.
"I'm Blackjack," said a small yellow dog.
"I'm Squeaky," said a cat with long dark fur.
"I'm Wheezer," said a dog with a long snout.
"I'm Grover," said a cat with gray spots.
"I'm Tiger," said a brindle hound.

Jeannette petted them all.

"**Suffering snowballs,**" she said. "This is a bad Christmas Eve for all of us."

Then Jeannette had an idea. A good idea. **A great idea.**

Jeannette poked around until she found some old clothesline. She made a lasso of it, and threw it around the chimney of the building.

She was back in a minute with the empty sack. **"Everyone hop in,"** she said.

Even for Jeannette, it was hard to climb back up to the roof with a sackful of cats and dogs. But she made it. She harnessed the dogs and cats to the sleigh with the clothesline.

"I'm back in business!" she cried.

"On Blaster, on Blackjack, on Wheezer and Grover.
On Tiger, on Squeaky, on Caesar and Rover!"

Up rose the sleigh. Off it flew, to every rooftop that waited for it,
until the sun began to catch up to it and Jeannette was done. Then back
they all flew to the North Pole.

The reindeer came trotting out of the barn at the sound of the barks and meows coming down from the sky. They stared as the sleigh landed gently in the front yard. Santa Claus tore open the window and threw up the sash. He smiled at what he saw.

"Hey, everybody, meet Santa's new team," Jeannette said.

She untied the dogs and the cats and opened the front door. Blaster and Blackjack, Wheezer and Grover, Tiger and Squeaky, Caesar and Rover all bounded in past the reindeer.

Jeannette started the fire. She put out milk and meat for everyone. "This is a nice place you've got here," said Caesar, licking his whiskers.

Jeannette **smiled.**

"**Welcome home,**" she said, "**and Merry Christmas!**"